A serial killer in training…

Perrin chuckled every time he thought of the trademark smile. It was as if the prey was glad they were dead because they left the world with a smile on their face. Hilarious!

Now here he was apprenticing in serial murder under the tutelage of his expert father who started his education by instructing him about the rules: no sexual contact with the prey, only take prey that live alone, and only take prey over the age of forty, preferably over fifty.

It was like Oslo often said, "Spinsters lives were worthless."

Tales of
Twisted Crime

R.G. Crossley

53RD STREET PUBLISHING

Dedication

For Rita who makes living wonderful.

Table of Contents

Introduction

I sit here in my office writing this introduction wondering how this marvellous journey started. The truth is my writing life started more than ten years ago when I first met Kristine Katherine Rusch and Dean Wesley Smith, two professional writers who became my teachers and my mentors. Eight years ago I made my first professional sale and it has been repeated many times. A first sale is wonderful experience and something you will never forget no matter how many sales you make.

It has been quite a journey so I thought this collection of mystery would represent my journey as a writer.

In this collection you will find stories about detectives and criminals, serial killers, and victims of crime. This is a diverse collection which I hope you will enjoy. If you find these stories entertaining keep an eye out for more of my stories since I love to share them with you.

If you want to contact me, look for me on Facebook and Twitter or through one of my websites. I'd love to hear from you.

R.G. Crossley
April 2013

R.G. Crossley
Presents
Tales of Twisted Crime

Published by 53rd Street Publishing

Logo image by:

Engraver | Dreamstime.com

ISBN 978-1-927621-15-8

© Wayne Mckown | Dreamstime.com

This is a work of fiction.
The persons and situations are products of the author's
imagination.

Drip!

Drip!

The green glow from the cheap radio alarm clock said it started at two a.m. precisely. A deafening drip forced Will Aston's red-rimmed eyes open and his rail-thin, pasty body to bolt upright on the lumpy, uncomfortable mattress.

Somewhere a dripping tap had interrupted his already tenuous attempt at slumber.

It had taken him five hours and five hundred miles to find this isolated motel off route seventy-three. He was desperate to find peace and quiet and sleep.

Now the drip had ruined everything.

First there was one, then two, then more in an ever-increasing crescendo. It began to sound like a steel drummer was playing inside his head.

Will hung his head in his hands, his naked body coated in a sheen of stale sweat.

Drip!

The thin white bed sheet clung to him like plastic kitchen wrap.

It's hot. Too hot.

The temperature outside was nearly ninety. Even at this time of night the dust covered air conditioner stuck in the window of the ancient motel room didn't work. It was likely much hotter in the room.

The wizened motel manager a man with a fringe of grey round his bald head, who looked to be as old as the outside temperature, told him the reason the air conditioner didn't work was due to the rolling black outs that frequently plagued this part of the country. Of course, Will didn't believe him.

The ancient springs in the mattress squealed in protest as he lowered his bare feet to the thin maroon carpet beside the bed.

They probably heard me in the next county.

He padded into the tiny kitchen to check the kitchen sink tap first. He ran a finger round the spigot and found it was dry. He next checked the bathroom. The sink then the shower and the spigot in the bath tub. They too were dry.

Odd. Where was the dripping tap?

He turned on the bathroom light.

Normally his night vision was sufficient for him to move around in a darkened room, even a pitch black one, but he needed to find that dripping tap if he was going to get any more sleep tonight.

He had an important sales meeting tomorrow and his boss, Mr. Walters, would be very unhappy if he missed the meeting. The Tri-State Automotive Parts and Repo account was the crème de la crème in his company. As vice-president of sales it was his job to keep this important client happy.

They bought seventy percent of the replacement lamps for auto headlights that his company Steven Lamps sold, and if they lost the account then most of the current jobs in the company. Mr Walters would of course fire him if he failed.

Why am I always getting distracted by such minor crap as dripping taps when there are far more important things to worry about._

Will stood over his Samsonite suitcase sitting open atop the stand he'd unfolded when he'd arrived.

He selected a pair of swim trunks his wife, Maggie had packed for him. Not that he had time to swim, but she always said he should be prepared for anything. He slipped first one leg then the other into the purple and orange nylon trunks and pulled the suit up past his narrow hips to his waist.

Drip!

His naturally dark curls were flattened by the pillow and the perspiration had so twisted his hair out of its natural shape he was certain he looked sufficiently scary to anyone he might meet into outside. He paused to listen. In the silence he heard unmistakable the dripping, rhythmic pattern drumming away to its own beat.

He sighed and then slipped on his tanned simulated leather walking shoes over his bare feet. He thought of putting on a shirt but decided not to bother. The night was warm and he'd only be out of the room for a few minutes anyway.

He stepped onto the covered wood walkway outside his room and was greeted by a burst of crickets chirping happily as if in greeting.

Great. More noisy critters to keep me awake the rest of the night.

He hesitated.

Funny, why didn't I hear them before now? They must've been here. Maybe I just didn't notice them.

Will moved toward the stairs leading to the ground floor and the parking lot beyond. He made sure the door was closed firmly by pulling hard on the imitation brass doorknob. The sound of the dripping tap seemed louder in the direction of the parking lot.

There was a single streetlight illuminating the parking lot. The blub cast a faded burnt orange color across the lot. Will knew his lamps and bulbs so he knew one when it was sorely in need of replacing.

As he reached the top of the stairs he could see the motel's office with its darkened windows and shredded curtains hanging like cheesecloth on either side of the window facing the parking lot. There were three other vehicles besides his in the parking lot. A white Buick Century, a silver Jeep, and a black Ford pickup parked in separate corners of the lot. The air was rife with the odor of gas and oil.

His '87 Skylark wagon was the farthest away. He'd had the car for years. Due to its two hundred plus thousand miles it wasn't worth much to anyone but him. It was the one possession he loved more than Maggie. Not that he'd ever tell her.

The dripping echoed from the foot of the stairs ahead. Once at the top of the staircase he spotted a rain trough with an old-fashioned hand pump hung over it he surmised must originate at an underground well.

He walked down the rickety wooden stairs. The worn stairs creaked sharply with every step. He winced with every footfall.

Please don't collapse now.

Drip!

Glancing toward the office he was startled to see what was obviously a light from a flashlight in the motel office's windows. He paused and held his breath afraid he'd woken another light sleeper like himself.

The yellow beam of light from the flashlight moved round the room pausing as if someone were searching for something.

He shrugged. Whoever it was it was none of his business.

He continued down the stairs until he reached the cracked cement pad at the base. He approached the rain trough.

It was constructed from an old oil drum cut in half then soldered together to form the trough. Sure enough the pump spout was dripping slowly splashing against the side of steel drum with a deafening splatter. At least it seemed deafening to him.

The drum half's were rusted away at the bottom so whatever water attempted to accumulate leaked into the ground beneath the barrel.

Will gazed at the pump handle and saw that it was stuck partly open. That explained why it was dripping. He placed one hand on the pump handle and pushed hard but it didn't budge. It had obviously rusted in place some time ago.

Odd, why did it start to drip only now?

He gripped the handle in both hands and struggled to move it. After nearly popping his hernia he managed to close the lever. Beads of sweat now covered his lean frame. He was gasping for breath.

The dripping had finally stopped. Mission accomplished.

Will smirked and rubbed his hands together in satisfaction. It was only then he noticed his hands were covered in orange rust, and the metallic smell made him feel a little nauseous. He definitely wasn't cut out for manual labour.

He glanced toward the office again and saw the beam from the flashlight was gone. The owner of the flashlight should've changed the bulb in that baby a long time ago. Even with fresh batteries the bulb was going to burn out very soon. He knew his bulbs.

He shook his head and headed back to the wooden stairs to return to his room. He'd be able to sleep now. He paused at the bottom of the stairs. The crickets had gone silent again.

Good, I'll be able to get some sleep after all.

He hurried up the stairs, accompanied by the musical creaks the boards protesting under his weight. Finally he arrived at the door to his room. He turned the door handle only to find the door locked.

Drip!

He tired it again without success. *I must've locked it out of habit.*

He patted down the pockets of his swim trunks and realized he didn't have the key. Now, he'd have to wake the old man and ask for a spare key. His face felt warm as embarrassment swept over him.

He was nearly naked in the middle of the night. How would he explain what he was doing out here at this hour? A grown man kept awake by a dripping tap. The old guy would think he'd lost his marbles.

The Vice President of sales wasn't supposed to get himself into such dilemmas. What would Mr. Walters think if he saw him right now?

Will sighed and chuckled. If Walters were here he would of course fire him. But his boss was hundreds of miles away.

When Walters bought the company from Maggie's father, Hiram W. Steven, one of the conditions of the sale was that his son-in-law be guaranteed a job for as long as he wanted it. Walters had been itching to find a way to rid of Will ever since that day five years ago. Now Walters may have the excuse he needed.

If he ever found out, which he wouldn't.

He retraced his steps to the top of the staircase and peered through the gloom into the motel's darkened office.

The bulb inside the street lamp was blinking intermittently now threatening to go out altogether.

Will hurried down the stairs barely noticing the creaking this time. The crickets were still silent as if they were waiting for something.

As Will stepped to the cement pad at the foot of the stairs the parking lot and the motel were abruptly plunged into inky darkness. With a burst of light as bright as a camera's flash going off the street lamp had finally gone out. There was no moon.

The only light available now was the sea of stars overhead. Will waited until his eyes adjusted to the meagre light. His night vision kicked in and soon he was able to find his way toward the office. As he neared the office door he noticed it was slightly ajar.

Odd. Things that were odd were beginning to pile up. *I've a bad feeling about this.*

He stepped to the door and pushed on it lightly with his finger tips. The surface of the wood felt like it had been freshly painted. The door swung open noiselessly on well-oiled hinges.

Maybe the old guy was finally fixing up the place? Will shrugged. *About time.*

The office was in total darkness. Taking in a breath he stepped inside nearly tripping over something lying on the floor.

Drip!

It was a large lump that looked vaguely familiar to him. He dropped to rest on his haunches to study the lump more closely. He gasped when he realized the shape was human.

His breath caught in his throat and his heart began to beat faster. Maybe it was a dead body? His mouth dried. He licked his dry lips. *Oh, crap. I don't feel so good.*

He rested one hand on the floor to steady himself and his fingers touched something sticky and warm. He froze with a rush of fear. Was that blood? The smell of iron filled his nostrils. A wave of nausea came over him. He stood up like a shot and panic raced through his mind.

What should I do?

He stood for what seemed like an eternity glued to the floor his mind racing with possibilities. The flashlight person must've been the killer. Maybe he was still around here somewhere.

Squinting in the darkness Will could make out the reception desk.

That's it. I'll call the cops. They'll know what to do.

He hurried to the reception desk his trembling hands fumbled around until he found the telephone. It was one of those old dial type phones.

He hadn't seen one of those in years.

He lifted the receiver to his ear and heard the thundering sound of silence.

A bead of sweat trickled down his back. The starlight coming through the front door was the only illumination. He could make out the body of the old man now lying on his side. He recognized the thin sweater the guy had on when he'd first seen him.

Will's eyes went wide when the old man moaned and rolled on his back his arms falling wide away from his wizened body. He was still alive.

Will dropped the receiver onto the desk. It landed with a thud. He then quickly moved to kneel beside the old man. "Are you okay?" he said his voice shaking.

Will rolled his eyes. *I'm an idiot.* Of course the old man wasn't okay.

The old man must have been shot or stabbed or something. And if the attacker was still nearby then he might be next.

Will decided to return to his room and barricade himself inside until help arrived. He paused. He couldn't leave the old man here. He might bleed to death.

From what he recalled during those monotonous first aid courses, Mr. Walters made him attend at the plant with the assembly line workers, Will knew he shouldn't move an injured man.

Drip!

But then again what choice did he have? The old man would die here regardless.

Will moved behind the old man and lifted him by his armpits. Blowing out his cheeks and puffing he managed to raise the old man enough so he could drag him by his heels.

The old man was like a dead weight but he managed to drag him outside the office. The old man moaned softly as he dragged him.

Once outside, Will eased him to the ground. Then bent over at the waist and drew in deep breaths, his arms trembling from the exertion and the sweat pouring off him.

Manual labour really isn't one my strengths.

When his breathing became somewhat regular he again reached under the old man's arms and began to drag him to the foot of the stairs where he once again eased him to the ground.

As he struggled to catch his breath he gazed around and was assured to see he was alone. The silence surrounding him was suddenly not as welcoming as it had once been. In the last several minutes it was if as if his world had suddenly been turned upside down.

From his stooped position he lifted his eyes to gaze at the stairs before him.

It might as well be Everest.

He wondered how he would get the old man up those stairs. The old man had stopped moaning, but he could see the man's chest rising and falling so he knew he was still alive.

"Here goes nothing," he murmured under his breath.

He reached under the old man's mans arms and heaved him up. He shifted the weight until it felt about the right balance then backed toward the stairs.

He managed to gradually climb up the stairs. The squeak of the tortured echo off the buildings surrounding the parking lot. As he climbed he looked over at the lot and nearly dropped the old man. He counted the vehicles. One was missing.

The silver Jeep was gone. How could that be? He hadn't heard an engine start while he was in the office. He looked around frantically as he negotiated the last few steps and arrived at the top of the stairs. His thin arms trembled as he eased the old man onto his back then collapsed to his knees breathing hard, partly with excretion, partly with fear.

Something was wrong about all this. His instincts were sending him warning signals.

It was like that time Ernie Walls wanted him to ride with him and Harold to the soda shop when he was seventeen.

Drip!

His two friends died in the car accident on Highway Seven when Ernie's brakes failed. Somehow he knew something was wrong and said that he didn't want to go with them.

It was no time to stop now they were almost at the room. He rose to his feet and again grasped the old man and began again to drag him to the room down the walkway. A soft moan escaped the old man's lips.

"Shush," whispered Will. His voice sounded harsh to his ears, but the old man stopped moaning right away.

He stopped outside his room door and eased the man to the thin, rough all-weather carpet covering the two-by-fours of the walkway. It occurred to him the worn carpet smelled of oil.

Again another irrelevant fact. He grimaced at the thought.

Maybe Mr. Walters was right. Maybe he should quit before he was fired. He could always go back to selling used cars. It was something he'd done to pay his way through business school. He'd not been the most successful car salesman but he'd managed to leave school debt free. All things considered he'd done okay.

Maggie's father had offered him the job at Steven Lamp based on his track record at the car dealer so it certainly counted for something didn't it?

Will reached for the doorknob when he realized he forgotten to get the spare key from the office. Now he'd have to go back and get it.

With one hand he wiped the rivulets of sweat running down his face and contemplated his next move. He shrugged. He would just have to risk going back to the office for the key.

If only the old man were conscious he wouldn't have to search the place to find the spare keys to the rooms.

When he'd checked in the old man had disappeared into a backroom and reappeared with the key in hand. It had one of those oval shaped moulded plastic key holders attached with the name and address of the motel engraved on it and a request to drop it in the nearest mailbox if found.

His options were limited. He left the old man unconscious outside his door and headed again for the stairs. He just made it to the ground level when suddenly night turned into day.

He was surrounded by a powerful beam of white light. He closed his eyes to the dazzling light and was frozen in place like a fly caught in amber.

Drip!

He raised one hand to shield his tearing eyes from the blinding white light just as he heard the roar of a motor spring to life. The growl of the obviously powerful engine was off to his left.

His instincts told him whoever was behind those headlights wasn't a friendly. He recalled the general direction of the office and decided to make a break for it. He could've gone back up the stairs, but with his suddenly limited eyesight he probably have tripped and broken something on the way up. It had to be the office.

He broke into a run. His legs felt as if they were mired in quicksand. The effort he'd expended carrying to old man up the stairs had made them weak.

The engine noise increased followed by the sound of tires spinning on the gravel. There was a roar of an engine. *The vehicle was headed at me? Why?*

His heart pounded in his chest. He blinked to clear his vision and was thankful when the office door was much closer than he'd thought it was.

In sheer desperation he launched himself into the air and landed heavily on his stomach knocking the wind out of him as he landed on a carpeted floor.

I made it!

He rolled over and gasped to drag air into his tortured lungs.

There was a sudden the crunch of metal and splintering of wood as the vehicle that had been chasing him crashed into the doorway behind him.

Will covered his head with his arms. *Oh, crap. What the....*

The office was suddenly flooded with bright white headlights followed by the sound of a car horn stuck on. The engine gasped, coughed roughly then died. The bleating car horn continued.

Will's head swam and he lost consciousness.

***

When Will woke he found a smiling male face above him looking at him. The man wore a blue pin striped suit and matching tie over a white shirt. His cherubic clean shaven features, replete with rosy cheeks, and flashing hazel eyes crinkled at the corners.

Is this was my maker looks like? He gazed into the friendly face.

"How are you feeling Mr. Aston?" said his *maker.*

Will then noticed a shiny gold badge in a black leather wallet sticking out of the left breast pocket of the man's suit. This was a cop *not* his maker. *Another stupid idea.*

"Huh…okay, I guess…" Actually he felt like he'd run a marathon.

Drip!

Not that he knew what that felt like, but his muscles ached and his head hurt so he assumed it. He was lying on a soft bed. He realized it was an ambulance stretcher.

"Do you think you can answer a few questions?" said the cop. "I'm Detective Zale."

"Yeah…I think so." It was really the last thing he wanted to do right now, but what choice did he have?

"Good," said Zale. The cop pulled out a leather encased brown notebook from his suit pocket. He flipped some pages back pausing to study some of his notes. His chubby features were transformed by the occasional frown. Zale then smiled slightly as he shifted his gaze back to Will.

"Do you know a Ronald Walters?"

Will nodded. "Yeah…huh…he's my boss…"

"Was," interrupted Zale with a slight smirk.

Will's eyes went wide. *Mr. Walters? What happened?* "What do you mean?"

"Sorry to break the news to you, pal he's dead. In fact, he tried to run you down with that Jeep."

Zale nodded to the door to the motel's office, which was framed by sunlight. There in the center of the doorway was the crumpled shaped of the silver Jeep he'd seen in the parking lot last night. Its front grill and hood were twisted out of shape as it someone had taken a sledgehammer to it.

"I don't understand…." said Will.

Zale continued in his matter-of-fact way.

"From what we can tell, Walters came here last night hoping to murder you. He knocked out the manager of the place, then tried to run you down with the Jeep." Zale paused and looked thoughtful. "Something I don't understand though why were you out here in your swim trunks? This motel doesn't have a pool."

My boss…tried to kill me?

Somehow, Walters found out about him being an extremely light sleeper, so he must've turned on the dripping tap knowing it would wake him.

Walters couldn't very well sneak into his room without drawing attention to himself so he'd waited until the motel was quiet then made sure the pump handle was open just enough to cause a drip.

Then he'd waited for him to come down and turn it off. The manager must've heard him and come to investigate and Walters knocked him unconscious.

"How's the old man?" said Will suddenly worried about the old guy.

Zale waved away his concern is if he were shooing flies. "Don't worry about him. He's at County General. They tell me he's gonna be fine. He's a strong old bugger. And smart too."

Drip!

Will gave him a quizzical look. Zale chuckled lightly, his sandpaper coloured eyes dancing.

"He'd just replaced the doorframe to the office with steel reinforced beams. They've had a number of break-ins around here and they'd lost some cash so he was in the process of renovating the office to prevent thieves from jimmying the door. Good thing for you. Otherwise that Jeep would've come shredded the wooden frame as if it were tissue paper…"

A blond haired male cop in his neatly pressed brown sheriff's uniform interrupted Zale to whisper something in his right ear. Zale looked surprised. His bushy eyebrows arched on his forehead.

"Are you sure?" The blond nodded his expression grim then he turned and walked away leaving them alone.

Zale turned back to face Will looking embarrassed his cheeks were crimson. "Mr. Aston, we've identified the other victim in the Jeep…"

"There was someone else with him? Who?"

"Margaret Aston."

Will felt a wave of shock fall over him like a tidal wave.

Maggie? Maggie was involved in this mess? How could that be?

The emergency sales trip was a ruse. Maggie and Walters must've been lovers and they wanted him out of the way.

How could I be so stupid, so blind?

He thought back and realized it explained everything. How else would Walters know he was such a light sleeper? They were both dead. They'd paid for their betrayal with their lives.

"All this from a drip," he murmured.

"What?" said Zale.

"Nothing — nothing important."

A Perfect Crime

BIG PETE SCRATCHED HIS BUTT ABSENTMINDEDLY as he stood in the crowded subway train headed uptown. An elderly lady seated behind him made an *ewww* noise he ignored.

Teleporters were too expensive on his limited income. He was forced to rely on the squeaking, bone-rattling cattle cars that made up the subway as his transportation of choice (or lack of choice).

These days every subway car was filled to the max with a seething, stinking mass of humanity all day long. The so-called *rush-hours* of the past were just that, they were in the past.

He smirked. "This here's a condition that's gonna change, and soon," he mused. His fingers tightened around the briefcase's handle in his right hand.

"What's so funny, man?" said a greasy-haired, meghead standing next to him.

The puke's sweaty armpit was almost in Pete's face. He had the appearance of one of those punks who was plugged into a heavy metal I-Pod Implant to listen to his music all day. If you could call that *noise* music.

Pete preferred the classics; the Stones, Marvin Gaye, Avril Lavagine. Any music was preferable to the junk this kid no doubt listened to twenty-four-seven.

The purple rooster ridge atop the punk's smooth pink head looked like implants. Or maybe his hair had been genetically altered prior to birth. Who knew anymore, and more important why would he care?

"Nuthin' that's any of yore bizness, punk-ass," said Big Pete, his inky gaze traveling up and down the younger man as if he was eyeing a sidewalk turd.

The younger man's eyes shifted to a look of concern. It had obviously dawned on him he had no idea who he was talking to. And while he was a head taller than Big Pete the older man's arms were heavily muscled, and his wide chest stretched his tight dirt-brown tee shirt to reveal the ridges of an equally muscled torso.

Pete fought the urge to chuckle at the guy while he kept his eyes fixed on the younger man's face that was becoming visibly paler with each passing second. Pete always enjoyed the way blood ran from the face of anyone who challenged him.

"Sumthin' wrong?" asked Pete.

The punk shook his head then averted his eyes to stare at the floor of the subway car.

Pete smirked again and went back to thinking about his part in Armand's plan. It was the perfect plan for a perfect crime.

***

Pete arrived outside the Excitement Corporation towers whistling a Stones tune to anyone who had no choice but to listen. He was off key as usual, but he didn't care. Naturally, he failed to notice passersby who lacked an appreciation of his musical talents.

He stopped and gazed upward at the sixty stories of glass and steel tower that housed the world headquarters of the company that was about to define his future. And make him and the others the richest people on the planet.

He entered through a set of revolving glass doors and made his way to the executive elevators to the left of the two identical rows of regular lifts. These were the ones reserved for company executives.

A burly guard, replete with regulation crew cut, and a well pressed blue and gray uniform, stood with his large muscular arms crossed over his massive chest. His bright blue eyes were fixed on the fireplug-shaped male headed for his position. Pete saw the slight twitch of the guards neck muscles.

This was the signal to his backup to join him right away.

Good for him, thought Pete. *He smells trouble with a capital T when he sees it.*

As he arrived in front of the guard a wide smile crossed Pete's swarthy complexion. "Hi."

"Sir." The guard nodded keeping his eyes fixated on Pete. His large hands were folded over each other in front of him as if he were guarding his family jewels. "May I help you," said the guard, the timber of his voice surprisingly high-pitched. His eyes were narrow as Pete watched the man's arms tense, and his booted-feet make those small measured moves to plant himself as if he were a human version of the classic brick wall.

"Big Pete Rustica to see Armand Takly."

The guard's thick dark eyebrows rose slightly upward on his dusky forehead. Pete knew that was because he wasn't the usual class of visitor that visited the Vice-President of Development for the largest Personal Recreational Interface Experience manufacturer in the world. The PRIE was the first and best system ever made.

It was the Blu Ray to the DVD of this generation. Brilliant marketing and a fairly reliable system of making customers dreams come true had made tens of billions of dollars in profits for everyone involved.

Armand Takly had been the chief systems architect of this technological miracle, and rumor was he was about to be arrested on trumped up fraud charges. When he was convicted — and he most certainly would be — his stock options would be revoked. And his bank accounts would be raped, leaving him a penniless pauper rotting in a jail cell.

Not that Armand wasn't guilty.

Every corporate executive was guilty of something. It was just that Armand thought he was made of Teflon, untouchable. He made the mistake of trusting his partners in crime.

Unbeknownst to his enemies, Armand had a safety net. His spies were in every boardroom and office in the company. He had his own plans to become very, very, *very* rich in the process. But he needed help.

This was where Big Pete, Tiny Murdoch, and Maurice "The Leech" Lévesque came into the picture.

When they were kids Maurice, and Armand attended school together in a small village in France. A fact scrubbed from company records, because if the company found out he was once associated with a notorious jewel thief he would never get away with what they were about to attempt.

Safety nets were important.

Maurice had never been caught — or even under suspicion by the authorities — for his illegal activities. Consequently, he could travel with complete anonymity anywhere in the world. Big Pete and Tiny were the worker bees of this operation.

They did all the heavy lifting and were well compensated for their part of the many successful robberies planned and executed by Maurice and his team.

The expert thief's policy was to steal from the rich who kept their valuables *off the books*. Insurance agents and the police wouldn't be looking for the perpetrators of the crimes. They didn't even have any idea where to begin looking if they pulled off each heist as planned.

It was a convenient and lucrative operation for all involved.

Of course, this didn't guarantee there weren't people looking for them. Many of these rich people were upset about losing their valuable trinkets. They would send private contractors to investigate. So far, no one had gotten close to the truth.

The truth was the rich victims often bought back their own merchandise at the next high priced auction even though the pieces looked very different from how they had last seen them.

Ironic, eh what? thought Pete with amusement.

He stood next to the cowed guard riding upward to the top floor in the high-speed elevator. When the guard checked with Armand's office the Vice President's personal assistant growled at him to stop delaying Mr. Rustica.

The elevator car was rife with the scent of the guard's cologne. It reminded Pete of rose water.

Kinda girly for a big guy like him. But what the hell. *I'm not his mother*.

The office over looked the city through a wall of glass spread out like a shining monument to man's ingenuity. The view took Pete's breath away. He had never been this high over the city.

Armand sat behind his glass desk. Tiny and Maurice sat in shiny red leather wing chairs in front of Armand's desk. Armand looked so regal in his five thousand dollar custom made suit. His black hair was streaked with traces of gray. His weathered face broke into a smile as Peter entered the room followed by Armand's assailant, a comely redhead dressed in a beige pantsuit who smelled of green apples.

"Thank you, Miss Taylor, please get a chair for Mr. Rustica —"

"Call me Pete, please," said Pete to Armand as Miss Taylor lifted and carried, with one hand, another of the red leather chairs away from where it sat against a wall then set it down next to Tiny's chair.

Impressive. Pete admired the woman's upper body strength. She probably doubled as Armand's bodyguard. Having a bodyguard that's easy on the eyes is a rich man's bonus.

Soon I'll be able to afford five who look like her.

Tiny's amused gaze followed Miss Taylor's rear end as she turned and left the room closing the door to the outer office behind her.

"My, my," breathed Tiny.

"Knock it off, Tiny," said Pete jokingly. "Ya'll soon be fightin' broads like her off with yore big stick."

Tiny snorted. "I'll show her a *big* stick awright —" To punctuate his point he grabbed his crotch.

"Will you two please cease the juvenile banter. We have serious work ahead," said Maurice dryly.

Pete and Tiny looked at each other and shrugged.

I hate it when he talks all high and mighty in fronta clients.

Some guys would think he was puttin' 'em down for not bein' so educated. Of course, Maurice and us we been makin' a lotta dough together over the years so he must be jokin'.

If there's one thing I'm good at it's readin' people."

"You bring the item?" said Armand, his tone anxious.

Pete wanted to laugh aloud, but he managed to contain himself. "Yeah. I have the *item*."

Guy musta seen one too many movies. Dork.

Pete slapped the hard-shelled black leather briefcase on the desk. He thumbed the catches on the left and right of the handle and they popped loudly with a metal-on-metal snap in the silence of the office.

Pete picked the data chip from a pouch designed to store and protect it then handed it to Maurice. A small plastic disk — about the size of a large washer — contained five trillion megabytes of data within its memory.

"Is this the one we need? As we discussed?" asked Armand.

Pete was getting seriously irritated by the guy, but he nodded any way forcing a placid expression to his face.

Maurice must have detected Pete's annoyance because he said, "As we agreed this simulation will allow us to practice the robbery countless times until we have it perfected —"

"How long will it take — I don't have a lot of time you know —"

Maurice held up one hand to silence his old school chum. Armand went quiet his eyes flitting back and forth over the three men sitting across from him.

Maurice cleared his throat then said, "We need the big lab on the seventh floor. It will take ten days to practice, then two to affect the robbery. The cops will buzz like angry hornets for several weeks afterward, but I'm not concerned with them. By the time they piece together what happened we'll be in a neutral country, safe from prosecution."

"Are there any neutral countries anymore?" said Armand.

A crooked smile crossed Maurice's face and his dark eyes flashed with humor. His fine boned hands smoothed his slate-gray dress slacks and he rolled his shoulders slightly beneath his gray tweed sport coat. "But of course, my old friend. I know all the right people in all the low places."

Armand eased back in his executive chair and laughed.

Pete stole a glance at Tiny. They both shrugged seemingly uncomprehending. What the heck were the two men were talking about? They were off the books. They weren't going anywhere as far as Pete was concerned.

**

Pete materialized within the walls of the vault. He stood frozen in place for a moment until the containment beam dissipated. Good thing too. If the quantum computer didn't reassemble your molecules in just the right place it was goodbye world and hello oblivion.

He looked around amazed at what he was seeing. It all looked so real. The vault even smelled of money. How freakin' real do these things get.

He'd always thought the PRIE's were designed for high-end gamers. Those types didn't need to steal. They just played at crime. It wasn't very long ago when people thought a video game could make someone commit a crime. Morons. The idea was just plain stupid.

Of course, the PRIE was much more than those old passive game systems. The gamer actually was able to interact with characters and change the outcome of the game. Safety systems were designed so the user wouldn't be hurt, but gamers could be shot, stabbed, or blown to bits, or make love to the woman of their dreams. It seemed as real to the gamer as the real world.

"Talk about your safe sex," Pete mused.

What you couldn't use the system for was to commit a crime. Even a simulated crime like the one they were attempting.

A black lab — one that would create anything for anyone for a price — created the program they were using to test the robbery. The lone downside was the safety protocols had to be taken out. Even holo-bullets can kill.

Oh well. Who wants to live forever?

Real people didn't have a use for such expensive toys. Million-billionaires bought these things. While there were plenty of them around Pete and Tiny certainly weren't in that category. The most they'd ever made in one year of working for Maurice was a hundred grand. Certainly not enough to buy an SUV never mind one of these expensive gadgets.

Armand's money paid for the black lab version and Pete knew it had taken most of his available cash. No wonder the guy was desperate. It was all or nothing. A real crapshoot. As it was for them.

They had never been on the cops radar given the attention this job was going to draw it would have to be their last. In the real vault, the hidden monitors couldn't be bypassed so their images would be flashed around the world when the robbery was discovered. They would just have to ensure they left the country ahead of the cops. Simple.

Yeah, right.

Of course, they planned to use the toy for far more than its designers originally intended.

They ran the robbery simulation seventeen times without one successful test.

The plan involved using a teleporter to materialize inside the vault containing the patents for every known piece of new tech that was acquired during contact with the Vetsa.

The Vetsa was an alien race that willingly shared their technology with Earth's industrialists. What the aliens didn't bargain on was the ruthlessness of Earth's most ambitious men and women.

The super rich wiped out all life on the aliens home world using their own technology and weapons. Not humanities finest hour.

A consortium of industrialists quickly applied for patents for the alien tech.

Humans now had access to teleporters, flying cars, guns that were encoded to one person's brain chemistry, and this holo-technology. The Personal Recreation Interface Entertainment (or PRIE) system made it possible to simulate any environment programmed by the user. Science fiction was now science reality.

Pete released the strap that held his .45 in place and held it up as the door to the outer vault area slide rapidly open and two guards rushed in wearing body armor. Pete methodically killed them both with one shot each in the center of their forehead. They dropped like two sacks of potatoes with hard thumps onto the tiled floor. Their drawn pistols skittered across the ties to stop at Pete's feet.

The iron scent of blood penetrated the air masking the smell of the money.

During the first two simulations, the two sim-guards had surprised him grazing his left shoulder in the resulting shoot out. He failed to notice they were wearing protective vests and had shot them each in the chest.

This slowed them but they kept coming and it had taken him several seconds to realize his mistake and take them down. Pain and the sight of your own blood were good teachers. He had to agree with Maurice. He was lucky.

Pete stepped over the two pistols just as Tiny materialized. He was wearing the body pack with the C4. Working quickly the two men squeezed the C4 from its packaging onto the center two titanium lined safety deposit boxes. The stuff looked like plumbers putty, but with more of a kick.

The boxes were eighteen inches by eighteen inches square. The patent certificates were secured inside. Pete licked his dry lips as they finished then he stuck in the detonators and set the timers for ten seconds.

He nodded to Tiny and they pressed their recall buttons simultaneously. The two thieves dematerialized and were standing on the lab floor looking at the large monitor affixed to one wall.

Within seconds, the screen became distorted, and as was the case seventeen times before, the floor beneath their feet trembled from the force of the blast. The screen settled down once more. Gray smoke obscured their view until powerful air exchange fans designed to remove smoke in case of fire sucked the smoke from the vault room.

Tiny glanced at Pete and smiled knowingly.

The two thieves pressed the buttons on their belts again and in the blink of an eye stood in the hazy air of the vault were looking at two safety despots boxes split open like fresh cantaloupe.

Instinctively Tiny reached inside the box nearest him. He froze and his face visibly paled. He stumbled backward holding his damaged hand. The boxes were booby-trapped.

Tiny groaned and blood dripped onto the floor from his nearly severed hand.

There was a large gash across the back of his hand cutting through the skin exposing the bone in his wrist.

This wasn't good. If Tiny's blood was found inside the real vault his DNA would lead the cops right to him. Could Tiny stand up to interrogation? Or would he talk to save his own skin?

Pete wasn't certain. *Nope this 'isn't good.*

"Hold." Pete and Tiny materialized back in the lab facing a distraught Armand and a very worried looking Maurice. Peter had never seen his boss look so worried.

"You okay, boss?" asked Pete. *Stupid question, Peter. Moron.*

"Very funny, Pete —" Tiny hit the floor hard and lay still. He'd lost a lot of blood and had no doubt fainted.

"What about him?" asked Pete, gazing at his friend laying unconscious on the floor curled in the fetal position.

"Take him to the infirmary on the first floor," said Armand curtly.

Pete shrugged and bent down to gather Tiny in his massive arms. He cradled him like a baby and then headed for the elevators.

***

"Test Nineteen," Pete said into the mike.

Within microseconds the massive computing power of the quantum computer than ran PRIE, the teleporter simultaneously set up the simulation, and he dematerialized.

As before, once in the vault he shot the two guards as if he was shooting at aluminum ducks at the carnival then set the charges and the timers.

Once the smoke from the explosion cleared, Pete stood staring at the two boxes. One contained a deadly trap that killed his friend — unbeknownst to them the blades in the trap were tipped with puffer fish venom — Tiny hadn't fainted he'd died. The other contained the certificates that were worth limitless wealth. They would be kings of all they surveyed.

For the first time in his life the question Pete faced was this worth it?

Closing his eyes, he ignored the box Tiny had put his hand in and instead reached inside the other one.

Nothing happened until his fingers brushed over paper. Hen snapped back his hand. His eyes flew open and frantically inspected his appendage for damage. With a deep sense of relief, he let out the breath he'd been holding and felt the urge to laugh.

Finally.

He quickly reached inside and pulled out the sim-certificates then slapped the button on his belt with the flat of his hand. Nothing happened so this time he gingerly pressed the button again.

Again, nothing.

What the — ?

An alarm began to wail and a wall of steel bars appeared from the ceiling blocking his exit via the door the two dead guards had come through.

Something was seriously wrong.

"Ah, Mr. Rustica I presume," said a deep baritone voice on the opposite side of the bars.

Pete walked toward the man his pistol drawn held waist level in front of him. Standing with an arrogant smirk on his lips on the other side of the bars was a man of medium height and weight wearing the uniform of the secret police.

In his youth, Pete had been a member of that organization so he knew the attire well. He also recognized the insignia on the collar. The man with the brown nearly trimmed beard, shot through with gray streaks, was a colonel.

"I hate officers," Pete murmured.

"I seem to have the drop on you, Colonel," said Pete waving the pistol to emphasize his point.

The colonel chuckled and crossed his arms over his chest. "Yes. I believe you do at that, Mr. Rustica —"

"Call me Pete."

"And you can call me Colonel Driver, *Pete*."

Pete feigned surprise. "Why so formal, Driver?"

Colonel Driver frowned. "Well you see, Pete, you and I are going to be spending a lot of time together."

It was Pete's turn to laugh. "I don't think so, Colonel. As you can see I have the gun."

Out of the corner of one eye, Pete saw a blur of movement coming from behind him. He attempted to turn but was too late. He felt a hard, painful snap against the back of his head and he fell on his side to the floor. His world exploded in a dizzying array of lights and spots that danced across his vision.

Dazed but still conscious he looked up at the Colonel who was now standing over him the bars having retreated into the ceiling.

"I don't understand," gasped Pete weakly. He detected the scent of the waxy polish coming from Drivers gleaming, calf-height boots.

"You're a deserter. You were convicted *in abstentia* by a military court. You will be taken into custody and serve your life sentence in Leavenworth."

"I have rights —"

"Deserters have no rights."

"But I committed the perfect crime."

"Mr. Rustica, there is no such thing as the *perfect* crime." Driver's eyes flashed. "Especially when a grief stricken woman is involved."

Pete's eyes looked puzzled.

Driver smiled mirthlessly. "Miss Taylor is one of our agents. She tipped us off what you and the others were doing. We're not interested in prosecution of the thievery, but I think you'll find your partners in crime will all be resting comfortably as wards of the state for quite some time."

Pete felt two sets of strong hands grab his arms and left him from the floor. His feet dragged so the two cops each held him up by placing one of his arms over their shoulders. They each had one around his waist to support his weight.

Driver was about to walk away when he paused and appeared thoughtful.

"And one more thing," he said slowly. "We would never have found out about you without Tiny Murdoch's death. I'm truly sorry about him, but as the French say, '*Ce la vie.*'

"Of course, the real loser in this little drama is Miss Taylor. She truly loved Tiny."

The Apprentice

Six weeks.

They spent six weeks planning the mission and the last thing he expected was a queasy stomach after all that time.

Ignoring his discomfort, Perrin ripped the strip of gray duct tape off the roll he had so meticulously pre-cut. This meant little effort was needed to pull off a strip just the right length.

The odor of the glue filled his nostrils forcing him sniff to try and clear the chemical smell from his nose and mouth. Like a bombardier centering the cross hairs on his target, he carefully applied the tape over the loose hanging mouth. He then pressed the tape hard into the soft flesh on either side of the mouth.

Its eyes remained closed, but the chest continuing to rise and fall was a sure sign of the familiar rhythm of sleep.

This sleep was artificially induced with the aid of the no-name chloroform he had purchased at Walgreen's, but it was still asleep.

They would need to wake it to complete their mission.

Perrin glanced up at the perspiration-dotted bald head of his father bent over it tying the knotted white rope around its pale wrists he had bought at Home Depot.

The rope was thin but strong. It was impossible to break unless you were big Arnold. This pudgy female with grey streaks shot through her artificially curled hair certainly didn't look like the strong type.

He could still detect the peroxide odor from the perm solution used to make its hair curly. Standing this close to it the new smell masked the trace odors left by the chloroform. Another very good reason to end its existence.

This was Perrin's first time since agreeing to become his father's apprentice.

He hadn't seen his Dad — he liked the sound of that word, 'Dad' because it filled him with a warmth unlike any he'd experienced toward anything or anyone for as long as could recall — since Dad and Mom deserted him years ago.

It had been a complete surprise when his father approached him at his $5.50-an-hour job at the Whistle Burger in the mall.

Since he didn't know the old man, he was neither happy to see him, nor angry with him.

He just didn't know this bald, heavy-jowled man so he also didn't care one way or the other.

He barely recognized the craggy features of the man from the pictures he kept in the tattered cardboard cigar box he carried with him as he moved from foster home to foster home while growing up. But it was the eyes that provided a clue to the man's identity.

Eyes the color of a cloudy sky were free of any emotion. It was as if the old man were death itself.

Yup, those eyes were a feature you could never mistake even from a picture.

When his father came to him he offered him an apprentice position with the telephone company where Oslo Hollis had worked for thirty years.

It took six months of working with Oslo and accompanying him on all sorts of service calls in his telephone company service truck before Oslo revealed his true intent.

Of course, Perrin had begun to suspect something strange was going on after Oslo caught him watching a documentary on television about a serial killer called the Smile Killer.

Perrin would never forget Oslo's burst of anger and demand he never watch such things again. Perrin's inner voice said Oslo's reaction was far more than parental concern for his not-so delicate sensibilities.

It was only when Perrin found the knife in Oslo's toolbox did he truly begin to suspect that his father was involved in something much more sinister than servicing telephones.

Naturally, Perrin burned to say something – in fact, he was bursting inside to say something, but he kept his suspicions bottled up inside. Until finally, Oslo said something over dinner one night.

Father and son sat silently eating across the small kitchen table from each other, their eyes avoiding the others. Sitting on the table in front of each of them was a microwave-heated TV dinner consisting of thinly sliced roast beef, peas and carrots, whipped potatoes, and apple cobbler.

Perrin had just popped some of the stringy beef into his mouth when he glanced up and saw his father was picking at his food.

Perrin paused and asked, "What's wrong, Dad?"

His father winced. "It's that obvious?"

Perrin put his fork down next to the aluminum tray and swallowed the piece of microwaved beef swimming in the bland gravy. "Yeah."

Oslo's emotionless gaze locked on his son's intense gaze. "I have something to tell you. Something important..."

Now this was getting interesting.

Perrin leaned forward his arms resting flat on the table his hands also flat on the table as if grounding himself. The sound of the cat-faced clock with its cheery smile hanging on the wall next to the white fridge seemed to be ticking louder in the thick silence that suddenly descended upon the room. His heart beat hard against his ribs as his excitement grew.

"I am..." Oslo hesitated. "I've never told anyone..."

"You can trust me, Da —"

Perrin felt a strange glow surge from his toes up his belly, landing finally in his throat where it choked his words off. He didn't want to spook his father.

Patience, Perrin.

Oslo nodded. He pushed back his chair with a loud scrape across the scarred linoleum floor. He went to the cabinet over the fridge where Perrin knew he kept a bottle of Scotch.

Oslo wasn't a drinker but he took out the bottle, and after retrieving a fresh glass from the cupboard next to the sink poured himself a healthy shot. Perrin noticed Oslo's hands were trembling.

Oslo downed the scotch in one swallow, coughed then turned and faced Perrin. His strong, pale hands gripped the back of his chair. He leaned into it and the frame creaked. His knuckles were white. "I'm the Smile Killer."

Perrin felt excitement well from within for the first time in his life. He was the proud son of Oslo Hollis the famous Smile Killer! The celebrated serial killer who had killed eight women over the past twenty years.

When the victims were discovered, they wore a frozen smile on their faces that the documentary had said the killer placed there by manually manipulating the face after death.

Perrin chuckled every time he thought of the trademark smile. It was as if the prey was glad they were dead because they left the world with a smile on their face. Hilarious!

Now here he was apprenticing in serial murder under the tutelage of his expert father who started his education by instructing him about the rules: no sexual contact with the prey, only take prey that live alone, and only take prey over the age of forty, preferably over fifty.

It was like Oslo often said, "Spinsters lives were worthless."

Perrin agreed. The sooner worthless spinsters were removed to make room for the more worthy in society the better off everyone would be. Theirs was a mission of mercy.

Of course, working up a profile on selected prey took a lot of work, and a lot of patience.

Carefully selecting the prey was first on Oslo's list.

He was very particular, not that Perrin would ever disagree with an expert. Oslo had killed eight of them over the last twenty years and had never been caught. In fact he had never even been questioned.

That was saying a lot. "The dumb ass cops," Oslo said, "They think all serial killers want to be caught!"

Perrin was forced to agree with his father's practical logic.

How stupid were these cops? After all, how was he supposed to complete his mission if he was in jail?

Obviously, the cops had watched too much television, or they believed in those mythic profilers. What a lot of nonsense.

Their motto was; so many to remove and so little time.

Perrin accompanied Oslo on visits to shopping malls and banks and even the airport hunting for potential targets.

Homeless prey were no good, they didn't have homes were they could work without risk of detection.

And just because the prey was at a bank or at the airport by themselves, even if they were in the right age range, didn't mean they were a perfect target. It seemed there were an awful lot of widows in the world.

"Look for wedding rings," Oslo instructed him.

Prey that was too wealthy was also no good. They often had drivers, bankers, or lawyers that would miss them. They weren't thieves so who cared how much money the prey had or didn't have. Only the mission was important.

If the cops found the prey too quickly it was a problem.

"Forensics," Oslo said, "the more rotted they were the harder it was for the forensic experts to find the minuet evidence they strained from the prey."

Spinsters had certain habits. They kept their bankbooks in their purses until they were asked for them at the teller. They wore clothes that, while they weren't shabby, weren't new either, and they were not what the beautiful people called attractive.

Usually they were in a hurry to get back to their small dog or pussycat. Oslo told him to listen for the prey to mutter something to themselves about their beloved pets. Concern over pets was a sure indicator the prey lived alone.

Widows were also no good because they often had children who checked on them. This could be messy and would result in the prey's discovery far too soon.

No. A good old-fashioned rotting corpse slowly beginning to smell as it ripened in the warm summer air, now that was a good kill.

Perrin warmed at the thought of the prey he was about to personally kill bleeding out then gasping its last breath as he stared at the prey hog tied on the bed. Its eyes were open, unfocussed, and sleepy. Gradually its eyesight must have cleared because its gray-green eyes popped wide with terror.

Good. Perrin grinned and raised his index finger to his lips as the prey began to protest in a low mumble behind the strip of duct tape covering its mouth.

It stopped and began to struggle against the rope securing its wrists and ankles. Fear and puzzlement swept over the pale skin of its face.

Perrin felt a thrill run through him as he stared at it. This experience was better than he had ever imagined it could be.

"Come here," said Oslo.

Perrin looked up to see his father standing at the foot of the bed, his bulky form silhouetted by the single side table lamp resting on top of a four drawer dresser against the wall behind him. It was the only light in the room. Perrin had made sure only one light was lighted in the tiny apartment bedroom.

Oslo said, "Minimal light made the setting eerie and terrifying for the prey."

Perrin had been resting on his hands bracketing the prey as he hovered over the struggling form lying on its back beneath him.

He pushed upward with his hands until his slight frame was off the bed. He pulled his black knit shirt down with both glove-encased hands as he stood up. He walked to the end of the bed to stand beside his father.

"You do it," gasped Oslo his breathing heavy.

Perrin was surprised his father was breathing so hard. Surely, they hadn't worked *that* hard…so far. In Oslo's right hand was a long-bladed, razor-sharp Bowie knife. Perrin knew it was heavy, very heavy.

Oslo kept the knife in the bottom of his toolbox wrapped in a worn piece of brown oil-stained leather. He told Perrin the weathered leather strip was from a vest worn by Buffalo Bill, but somehow Perrin doubted it.

He scanned the struggling prey dressed in her ankle-length cotton nighty. He felt the power that was his for the taking. It coursed through his veins. He was life and death. Life was his to give and his to take.

Lois Kildair. Spinster. Age sixty-three. Retired librarian. Three cats and a budgie in a gilded cage. Perfect. The perfect prey.

Perrin accepted the knife from Oslo and smiled as he gripped the heavy handle. The weight felt good in his hand. He moved toward the struggling prey.

***

Suzie White looked up from her computer screen where she had very nearly completed her report when Ozzie Wilson sat down heavily in his desk across from hers.

Ozzie was the old hand in their partnership. He'd been a homicide detective for fifteen years.

She'd only made detective five years ago. Three of years of that she worked burglary, until she was reassigned to homicide. Her dream job.

Ozzie was a large man who loved his donuts. She swore his pores oozed sugar and fat. He was sweating profusely when he sat down with a heavy sigh.

"Well?" asked Suzie her thin eyebrows high on her dusky forehead.

Ozzie may have an ample paunch hanging over his belt, and he might not be the best dresser in the room, but he had a sharp mind and good instincts. He was a good cop and she was glad when she was partnered with the Oz.

He looked over at her and smirked. "I think the kid's involved. I don't know how…yet."

Suzie's lips smiled but her eyes were deadpan. "The DA said we have to leave it alone. He's glad we got the Smile Killer."

Ozzie leaned back in his chair and chuckled coldly. "Yeah. Right. The guy had a heart attack while the boy was slicing and dicing the librarian with a Bowie knife." He shook his head as his expression became sad. "We didn't *get* anyone. Truth is Oslo Hollis dropped dead in our laps."

"What did the DA say was gonna happen to the kid we found at Kildair's place?"

Ozzie frowned and his bravado evaporated. "He's being locked up in the nut house up in Cherryville. And he'll be gettin' out some day...."

Suzie shook her head. "Yeah...it's hard to imagine. Only fifteen and he thought this guy Hollis was his father. Said he was Hollis' apprentice. I checked on him —"

She read from her report; "Perrin Dystry: parents, Fered and Carmella Dystry killed in a car crash in '96.

"As far as we can tell ever since then the kids pinballed his way through the foster home system. Now he's gonna live in a nut house for a few years." She shook her head. "He sure freaked when the paramedics told him Hollis had croaked. Good thing the black and white arrived right after the ambulance or we'd have two paramedics bodies to clean up."

Ozzie nodded. He crossed his feet on top of his desk and locked his meaty fingers behind his head then leaned back. "Yeah, kids can be so easily mixed up by bad parentental figures."

Yeah, thought Suzie as she turned back to study the photo of the kid in the file. *Especially when he thinks his father is training him in the serial killer apprenticeship program.*

On days like these she wondered if maybe she should have stayed in burglary division. She snapped the folder shut and dropped it in the to-be-filed bin on her desk on top of all the others.

She sighed. The captain had assigned them a fresh case half an hour ago.

On to the next case.

A Beautiful Friendship

THE AIR REEKED WITH THE THICK SMELL OF OIL and gasoline. The noxious, sickening fumes mingled with a hint of burnt gunpowder. The smells invaded Chase Valentine's nose leaving a vaguely metallic taste in her mouth.

Crouched uncomfortably behind a rusting steel drum she licked her cracked, dry lips. The mounting tension and the too-dry air had affected her more than she thought it would.

Rising slowly from her haunches, her muscles protesting every inch, she peered over the top of the drum into the inky darkness.

The loading dock was littered with oil drums, any one of which could be hiding an enemy or her target. Oscar Montoya had to be hiding in here somewhere. And she was going to have to find him.

Problem was Oscar was armed to the teeth. Odd how disgraced millionaires who hire beautiful private investigators object to being brought to justice when things go bad.

Releasing her cell phone from the holster on her hip, she flipped it open. The small LCD screen lit up, just the phone beeped loudly in the silence.

She cursed under her breath as the words *low battery* flashed repeatedly across the screen. "If only there's time —"

Her long fingers flashed across the illuminated keypad, *9-1-*. Her fingers hung frozen over the remaining one when the screen changed to *Have a Nice Day* then went dark. A disheartened sigh escaped between her lips. "Sorry, baby. I didn't have time to charge you."

The call informing her Montoya was hiding here arrived just as she arrived home form a stake out. She didn't have time to recharge it before she had to race to the warehouse. Her usual luck had failed her this time.

Placing the dead phone back in its holster she cursed herself again. Her ragged breath echoed in her ears. At least Oscar had stopped shooting.

Somewhere to her right in the darkness was, Rex Harper, her newly acquired partner.

Not that she needed a partner, but Oscar had hired them both without them knowing about the other, until ten minutes ago. Oscar obviously thought he'd play one against the other.

She gritted her teeth and a smirk played across her lips. *Wrong again, boyo.*

The cool handle of her Dad's 9mm Glock felt comfortable in her hand. When she'd inherited The Valentine Detective Agency after her father's death she'd assumed all his tools of his trade, including the reliable Glock.

Where the hell was Rex?

In the darkness, she skirted the field of oil drums then, keeping her head low, scurried like a spider pressing her back against a brick wall to her right and behind her. Always keep something between you and any possible enemies behind you, her dad used to tell her.

The bricks felt solid against her leather jacketed back. Her heart thumped in her chest. She willed herself to remain calm, but kept the Glock at the ready.

A sharp scrape that sounded as if it were almost beside her brought her internal sensors to full alert. Chase froze where she stood her breathing now rapid in her ears. She strained her hearing to catch any additional sounds.

A throaty voice whispered her name causing her heart leap into her throat and her index finger to tighten on the guns trigger. "Chase, it's me —"

"By God," she replied, her whispered words clipped with tension. "Damn it, Rex, I could have shot you —"

"But you didn't," said Rex with a hint of sarcasm in his tone.

The man was incorrigible, but that face...*oo la la*. With ice blue bedroom eyes, and wavy dark-brown hair Rexy boy he was just too handsome for his own good.

"Do you think we should get a cup of coffee after this case is over?" She heard Rex's deep voice coming from her immediate left. He was close. Too close.

Somehow, in the darkness, he'd managed to sneak up beside her without her realizing it. She chastised herself. This wasn't a good thing to happen to a detective. Dad would be disappointed. She determined she would do better in the future. But for right now....

"How can you be so calm?" she whispered.

"*My* cell phone is fully charged..." he paused then added, "I keep a spare with me when I'm on a case. And an extra suit of clothes in my car trunk. You never know when you'll need 'em."

Chase wondered why she hadn't thought of such obvious things. After all detective work meant long hours. It wasn't a nine-to-five job. She had a lot learn. If only dad were here.

Her thoughts were interrupted when the dead calm air was torn violently by the sudden appearance of a roaring helicopter that flew low over the steel corrugated storage sheds littering the docks visible form where they were hiding on the loading dock. A brilliant spotlight affixed to its belly forced Chase to squeeze her eyes shut. Her long blonde hair whipped about her head in the suddenly churned, rough air.

She raised her hands to shield herself from the violent down draft caused by the helicopters rotors. She opened one eye to see Rex signalling to the occupants with his snub-nosed .38. Rex was a cliché. Nobody carried snub-nosed .38's anymore. Who did he think he was Joe Friday?

He motioned to the sheds in the distance. That's where the most recent shots had come from.

When the helicopter disappeared from overhead headed for the sheds beyond her dishevelled hair settled around her shoulders once more. Chase was certain her hair must look as if she'd combed it with an eggbeater. Which in a manner of speaking was accurate.

The helicopters white spotlight speared the dock in a roving pattern hovering over the sheds and eight-foot high stacks of oil barrels searching like a bloodhound hot on the trail of its prey.

Finally, it settled into a hover like any good bird dog would do and pointed the nose of the aircraft downward its beam of white light bathing a row of three-high stacked steel drums.

Rex glanced at her with an easy casual smile splitting his handsome features. He pulled back his navy blue windbreaker revealing a trim torso and slipped his gun into the shoulder holster beneath the thin nylon jacket. "Well, I guess the cops are gonna take care of 'ol Oscar."

Just as he spoke three black and whites, no doubt filled with officers of the cities finest, came screaming onto the dock their red, blue, and white rollers flickering off the sheds. The three squad cars headed straight for the target painted by the helicopter.

Oscar appeared — his eyes wild and angry stood up from behind the drums with his empty hands held up in surrender.

Chase stared at Rex with a smirk on her lips. "Well, I guess we better get that coffee." She smiled at him and holstered her pistol on her hip.

Rex laughed and placed one muscular arm around her shoulder. "Ya know, Chase, I love the way you handle yourself. Maybe you and I should go into business together."

Chase nodded and ran one hand though her hair to smooth away the blonde strands that bracketed her face. "Yeah…maybe…"

"After all, your old man and I did some freelance work together a couple of years back. And I really love what you've done with your hair."

Chase couldn't help but laugh. Rex the charmer. But, Dad worked with Rex? Funny he'd never mentioned it.

She shrugged. *Maybe Rex and I would make a good team.* She glanced at him then smiled to herself. It felt right.

As Bogart once said, this is the start of a beautiful friendship. And maybe more, much more.

The Parrot of Doom

I HAD NEVER SEEN A REAL PARROT in the flesh (or should I say in the feather), before today.

From where I sat on the worn leatherette sofa in my partner, Morton Edge's, parents recreation room I stared at the brightly colored green, and yellow (but mostly green) parrot, with a mustard yellow stripe across his beak. The bird sat on a perch in a cage that appeared to be designed to hold the Count of Monte Cristo it was so big.

The parrot (Edge explained his name is Hercules) had been dropped off by a client, and we were to interrogate it.

"So what is the parrot supposed to tell us?" I asked.

Edge looked up from the romance novel he'd been reading, his hazel eyes free from emotion.

He rarely displays human emotion because he thinks it's a sign of weakness. I think it shows we're all human. I sometimes wonder if Edge is human because he sees the world in such a different way. Then again this is the reason he's so gifted at deductive reasoning, and so bad at human relations.

Human relations is my job at Razor and Edge Investigations. I'm the one who wears out his shoe leather.

"Razor, please refer to the parrot as Hercules. He understands our every word, and I'm told he's offended when referred to as an object."

Objectifying a bird? Now I really have heard everything.

"Huh, yeah, sorry, Hercules," I said, directing my words to the parrot staring back at me with one coal-black eye.

I almost jumped out of my skin when the parrot spoke. "No worries," he said. "Please call me Hercules."

"Uuuuhhh, yeah, OK." My cheeks grew warm. I couldn't believe it but I was embarrassed. I shifted my bony behind on the sagging sofa cushion. The darned thing is so old and ratty sometimes the springs press the flesh with the occupant. This old sofa is where the butt meets the road.

I gathered my rattled senses and decided I better speak to the parrot. "So, Hercules, what is it you're supposed to tell us?"

The reply was immediate. He shuffled along the perch farther away from me then said, "About Mr. Cunningham's affair."

Hercules was certainly clear, but I was confused. I'd missed something so I directed my next question to my partner. "Edge, I'm obviously out of the loop, could you perhaps explain what's going on, and why Hercules is here?"

Edge closed his novel, after slipping in a bookmark, then set the book on the end table next to his Barcolounger. "Do you wish to explain, Hercules?"

"After you, Mr. Edge."

Oh, brother. To this day I think Hercules was mocking me.

Edge nodded sagely. "Mrs. Cunningham contacted me asking us to follow her husband because she believed he was being unfaithful. She said she'd pay us any amount we asked for. I explained we do not take those kind of cases."

Though I knew he was right, I was disappointed we'd lost a paying client to a little thing like ethics. I frowned and glanced at the parrot sitting serenely on his perch then back at Edge.

"If you refused the case then why is the pa—I mean, Hercules, still here?"

"Because he knows something about Mrs. Cunningham's murder."

To say I was shocked by this revelation would be an understatement of the first magnitude. "What? Mrs. Cunningham is dead? So who brought us the bird?"

"Mr. Cunningham," said the parrot.

I paused to consider the information I had so far. Mrs. Cunningham calls us to hire us to follow her husband who she thinks is having an affair. She is then murdered, and her grieving husband brings us the bird. What? This is nuts.

"But why would Mr. Cunningham bring us the bird?"

Edge shook his head. "He didn't," my partner said matter of factly.

"I called Mr. Edge," said Hercules.

I gawked at the parrot. *He* called Edge?

Edge chuckled. "Sorry, Razor, I've been having too much fun. Please forgive me." He paused and his lips formed a crooked smile. "Hercules knew Mrs. Cunningham had called us and pressed the re-dial on the phone. He told me that he'd witnessed Mr. Cunningham killing his wife. He was indeed having an affair, and planned to run off with his lover.

"After Hercules called me I contacted Detective Aimes telling him I had spoken to a witness to a murder, and that the murderer was about to kill the witness."

"Too true," interrupted Hercules.

Edge smiled then continued. "I gave Aimes the address and the police arrived in time to catch Mr. Cunningham attempting to flee, and they saved Hercules from certain death."

"I'm the parrot of doom," said Hercules.

Parrot of doom? Oh, brother. who knew a parrot could be so dramatic. Then again it would make a good blog title.

"So back to my original question," I said. "Why is he here?"

"The Cunningham's adult daughter is flying in from Los Angeles tomorrow. She'll take Hercules back with her. We're looking after him until then."

"Oh." I eased back against the sofa cushion.

I snatched the TV remote off the scarred pine coffee table in front of the sofa. "Wanta watch some TV, Edge?"

"I like the Home and Garden Network," said Hercules.

I looked at Edge. "Edge?"

He shrugged. "Parrot's choice."

I turned the television on and changed the channel to the Home and Garden Network.

Parrots choice indeed. Stupid parrot's gonna be doomed alright.

About the Author

International selling author, Russ Crossley writes romance under the name R.G. Hart, mystery/suspense under the name R.G. Crossley, and science fiction and fantasy under his own. This year there will be re-issues the romantic comedies, Bachelorette: Zombie Edition by Champagne Books, and Antique Virgin by 53rd Street Publishing, paranormal romantic comedy, Zomopolis, and a new western romance entitled, The Fire In Their Hearts co-authored with R.S. Meger will be published in 2013 by Champagne Books. Also, look for another Aloha adventure, Bloody Betty Queen of the Pirates coming in the spring of 2013 from Champagne Books.

In addition the near future suspense novel, The Last Serial Killer by R.G. Crossley was recently released by 53rd Street Publishing in ebook and trade paperback versions.

He has sold several short stories that have appeared in anthologies from Pocket Books, St. Matins Press, at Smashwords, Amazon, and other e-retail sites.

With his wife, romance author R.S. Meger, he owns and operates a small press publishing company, 53rd Street Publishing. The company began in April 2011 and now has over one hundred e-book titles and a number of print titles, with more planned in 2012 and 2013.

He is a member of SF Canada and the Greater Vancouver Chapter of Romance Writers of America. He is also an alumni of the Oregon Coast Professional Fiction Writers Master Class taught by award winning author/editors, Kristine Katherine Rusch and Dean Wesley Smith.

To find a complete listing of his work check out his website http://www.rghart.com, http://russstory. blogspot.com.Razor's blog can be found at http:// razorandedge.blogspot.com

Feel free to contact him on Facebook or Twitter. He loves to hear from readers

Other books by the Author

Titles as R.G. Crossley

Short Stories

Razor and Edge Mysteries
The Kidnapping of Billy Buttons
String of Pearls
Death by Clown
Beggin' For Murder
Ragged Ice
The Grand Central Mystery
A Strange Case of Undead Murder

Non-Series Mysteries
A Day Without Sunshine
Mirror Image
Dangerous Waters
Cape Disappointment
Boomerang
The Watcher of Wayburn Street
The Apprentice
Drip!
A Beautiful Friendship and The Parrot of Doom
Robine's Diary
The Christmas Club
Loose Ends
Skullduggery
Splatter Pattern

It Takes Two

Anthologies
The Adventures of Razor and Edge:
Five Tales From The Quirky Detective Team

Novels
A Bad Case of Loyalty
The Last Serial Killer
Shear Murder

Titles as Russ Crossley

Novels
Attack of the Lushites
Revenge of the Lushites (coming soon)

Short Stories
Countdown
Shoeless Moe
Round Up At The Burger Bar:
The Story of Trixie Pug, Parts 1, 2, 3, 4, 5, 6, 7
Five Minutes
Blossom Queen, Barbarian
The Secret
The Family Line
End of the Flies
With Death You Get the Eggroll
The Penguin Sleeps With The Fishes
Only The Worthy
Hero For A Day
End of Empire

Strange Bedfellows
Big Business
A Perfect Crime
The Wise Guy and The Pirates
In Search of the Perfect Cup
T.I.N. Men
The Legend of G and the Dragonettes
The Incredible Mr. Fix-It
Lock Stock and Barrel
Divided Loyalties
Cave of Wonders
A Family Empire
Until We Meet Again
Dragon Rising

Presents Anthology Series
Five Tales of Urban Fantasy
Five Tales of Bizarre Detectives
Five Tales of Mystery and Suspense
Five Tales of Weird Fantasy
Spies, Detectives, & Heroes
Tales of Twisted Crime
Five Tales of The Unexpected
Tales From Space
10 by Russ Crossley
Round Up At The Burger Bar: The Story of Trixie Pug, Parts 1- 5 The Beginning
Worlds of Science Fiction and Fantasy
More Tales of Mystery and Suspense
Ladies of the Jolly Roger
Justice Served

Titles as R.G. Hart

Short Stories
Tikka's Big Day
"My Partner the Zombie" —
Hungry For Your Love Anthology
(St. Martin's Press)
Big Hairy Deal
One Red Shoe
A Bad Day in Lunden Texas
Hook Island
Grind Manor
Bloody Betty, Queen of the Pirates (coming soon from
Champagne Books)

Novels
Bachelorette: Zombie Edition
(from Champagne Books)
Antique Virgin
The Fire In Their Hearts
with R.S. Meger (coming soon from Champagne
Books)
Zomopolis

www.ingramcontent.com/pod-product-compliance
Lightning Source LLC
Chambersburg PA
CBHW020548130626
46552CB00007B/2806